Harold

Based on
The Railway Series
by the
Rev. W. Awdry

Illustrations by
Robin Davies

EGMONT

EGMONT

We bring stories to life

First published in Great Britain in 2016
by Egmont UK Limited
The Yellow Building, 1 Nicholas Road, London W11 4AN

Thomas the Tank Engine & Friends™

CREATED BY BRITT ALLCROFT

HiT entertainment

ISBN 978 1 4052 7978 9
62419/1
Printed in Italy

Written by Emily Stead. Designed by Claire Yeo.
Series designed by Martin Aggett.

The next day Percy stopped at the Airport. "My name's Percy," he peeped. "Who are you?"

"I'm Harold," said the helicopter. "With my **whirling** rotor blades, I can fly like a bird. Don't you wish you had some, too?"

"No," said Percy grumpily. "I like keeping my wheels on the rails."

"Engines are much too **slow**," Harold went on. "I can go **faster** than any of you!"

Before Percy could reply, Harold had flown away.

Percy puffed to the Quarry feeling angry.

"You look cross, Percy," said Toby the Tram Engine. "What's the matter?"

Percy told Toby what Harold had said about **helicopters** being faster than **engines**.

"That's not right!" Toby agreed.

As Percy puffed back to the Harbour, he heard the **buzzing** noise again.

"Look, Percy," said his Driver. "There's Harold. Let's have a race — then he'll see who's fastest!"

"Pip! PEEP!" whistled Percy, rushing after Harold. "We'll show him that wheels are best!"

Harold heard Percy racing on the rails below. **Clickety-clack, clickety-clack!** Percy was catching up with him!

"You'll never beat me!" Harold **whirred**. "I will land at the Airport before you reach the Harbour."

But Percy puffed bravely on. **"Hurry! Hurry! Hurry!"** he told the trucks.

The race was on!

Harold didn't think that such a little engine pulling a heavy train could ever beat him.

Then suddenly Percy puffed level with Harold.

Minutes later Percy's Driver called, **"We're in the lead, Percy!"**

Percy's wheels had never rolled faster.

"**PEEP! PEEP!** Goodbye, Harold!" Percy whistled as he raced ahead.

Harold looked down in surprise and hurried after him.

Percy's Fireman shovelled coal into Percy's firebox as fast as he could.

"This is hard work," said the Fireman. "I hope we beat Harold."

Up ahead was the Harbour Wharf. **"Nearly there!"** Percy's Driver called.

Percy stopped sharply before the buffers.
"Did . . . we . . . win the race?" he puffed.

His Fireman climbed onto Percy's cab. **"Yes!"**
he shouted. "Harold is still trying to land."

Percy blew his whistle happily. **"Pip! PEEP! PEEP!"**

He had shown Harold that engines were as fast
as helicopters!

"Well done, Percy!" Harold called. "What fine wheels you have!"

Percy felt happy from funnel to footplate!

Now when Percy hears a **buzzing** noise in the sky he doesn't mind at all. He always whistles to his friend Harold, and Harold hovers to say hello.

More about Harold

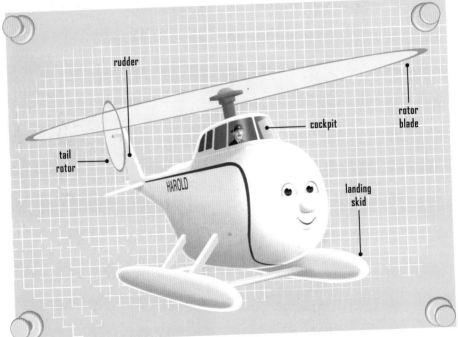

rudder

tail rotor

cockpit

rotor blade

HAROLD

landing skid

Harold's challenge to you

Look back through the pages of this book
and see if you can spot:

boat

sheep

lifebuoy

train driver

biplane

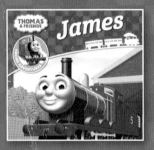